Anne Fine

Back on

WEIRD STREET

With illustrations by
Vicki Gausden

First published in 2018 in Great Britain by
Barrington Stoke Ltd
18 Walker Street, Edinburgh, EH3 7LP

www.barringtonstoke.co.uk

A CIP catalogue record for this book is available
from the British Library upon request

ISBN: 978-1-78112-788-9

Printed in China by Leo

CONTENTS

It was a freezing day, but Asim, Laila and I were sitting on the wall half way down Weir Street. We often meet there. Laila was telling us about a dream she'd had the night before.

"It made me think I'm going to get a letter with good news," she told us.

I said, "Don't get your hopes up, Laila. Dreams are just dreams."

"Not always, Tom," she told me firmly. "And especially not here – not here on Weird Street."

A shiver ran down my spine and I pulled my jacket tight around me. The real name of our road is Weir Street. It's called that because there is a stretch of river at the end that plunges down, fast and deep like a waterfall, over the old weir. But so many strange things happen between the weir and the other end of the road that we three have begun to call it Weird Street.

We share the stories between us. Asim said, "Laila is right. Sometimes dreams can tell you things." He turned to look at his sister. "Tell Tom that new story, Laila."

"What new story?" I asked them.

"I heard it yesterday," Laila said, "from Harper."

I must have looked blank because Laila reminded me.

"You know Harper. She lives in that tiny house next to the river. The one with the red door and the crooked chimney and the back garden full of hollyhocks. She came round to ask if we had any spare boxes."

"Why does she need boxes? Is she moving?" I asked. "I know her great-grandpa left her mum the house when he died. But everyone says that it's nasty and damp all year and floods almost every winter."

Asim said, "They say the cellar walls are always green with slime."

I shivered again, and not just from the cold. "Ee-ew!"

"Then she'll like her new house so much more," said Laila. "They're moving into Tinsley Lodge."

I was astonished. "Tinsley Lodge? But that big house must cost a *fortune*."

"She *has* a fortune," said Laila. "She got it from a dream."

I laughed. "I told you, no one gets anything from dreams – especially not money."

Laila looked at her brother. They both grinned. Then Laila said to me, "Wait till you hear the story that Harper told me."

So we all snuggled close on that cold wall, and Leila told us what Harper had said to her as they were looking for boxes ...

Tale 1

The Voice from Barton's Bridge

I've always slept like a log. Mum says I go out like a light and have done ever since I was a baby. I never lie there in the dark and count the hours.

Until this summer.

This summer, I started to hear a voice. Sometimes the voice woke me the minute I'd dropped off to sleep. Sometimes I heard it in the middle of the night. Sometimes it didn't wake me till it was almost morning. But it was always the same voice. An old man's voice. Soft. Almost like a whisper. And it was always saying the same thing.

"Look under Barton's Bridge."

The voice was inside my bedroom, but it never scared me. I think that was because it sounded so soft and kind. I even had the feeling that I'd heard it before, a long, long time ago. It always said the same words: "*Look under Barton's Bridge.*"

I'd never heard of Barton's Bridge, but in the end I looked on the big map in the library and found it. It's quite near. Just three miles away. Years ago, there was a bike factory called Barton's on one side of the bridge. That's all gone now, but everyone who lives close by still thinks of that bit of the road as Barton's Bridge.

So I cycled off one day to take a look. I chained my bike to a lamp-post and walked along the pavement under the bridge. The bridge is built with brick, so your footsteps ring out when you walk under the high arch, and, if you call, your voice comes back as an echo.

I looked around. There was the road, with cars whizzing past every now and again. There was the pavement I was walking on. A few weeds grew between the paving slabs. There were patches of moss on the bricks.

But nothing special. No reason for an old man's voice to send me here.

"OK," I told myself. "I've done it. I've looked under Barton's Bridge. And now I can go home and sleep without the voice waking me up."

On the way back to my bike, I saw a farm worker watching me from behind a hedge.

I said "Nice day" to him as I walked past.

But he just scowled and said nothing.

*

The voice came back that night. "*Look under Barton's Bridge.*"

I spoke back to the voice for the first time. "I've done that. I went today. There's nothing special there. Nothing at all."

It was as if I hadn't said a word. The voice just said again, as softly and as calmly as before, "*Look under Barton's Bridge.*"

I thought that maybe I had missed something. Had I looked closely enough at the bricks? What about the slabs of the pavement? Was there something hidden in the weeds or behind the moss?

So I went back. I left my bike in the same place and took my time. I spent nearly half an hour, and I inspected every inch of brick and pavement. I poked among the weeds. I peered up into the shadows under the arch of the bridge.

But there was nothing. Nothing! The bricks were solid. The paving slabs were firm, with no cracks. Nothing was hidden in the weeds.

So I went back to my bike. The farm worker was behind the hedge again.

"Not quite so nice today," I called to him.

He was as grumpy as before – just grunted and turned his back on me.

*

The voice was back that night. "*Look under Barton's Bridge.*"

"No," I said. "I've been there. Twice. And there is nothing there."

"*Look under Barton's Bridge.*"

I thought I'd go back one last time. I was sure I'd find nothing. But I so wanted the voice to go away. I didn't want the farm worker to catch me staring at the bridge again, so this time I went very early in the morning.

The farm worker was already there, behind the hedge. I saw him watching me, and after I'd spent a bit of time looking at everything under the bridge, I saw him walk through the farm gate and come closer along the road.

As soon as he was under the arch, he said to me, "You're here again! Why do you keep coming here to hang about under this bridge?"

I knew my answer would sound odd. But I didn't know what else to say, so I told the truth.

"I hear this voice in my dreams. It wakes me every night. It tells me to look under Barton's Bridge. That's all it ever says – '*Look under Barton's Bridge.*'"

The farm worker scowled. "You must be crazy," he said. "Or *stupid*. Everyone has dreams. Take me. For ten years now I've had dreams of a tiny house with a red door and crooked chimney. It's by a weir and it floods every year. The cellar walls are green with slime. I dream that there's a fortune buried under some hollyhocks in the garden. But it's a *dream*. I'm not so foolish as to go and look for it."

"I'm sure you're not foolish at all," I told the farm worker. "I'm sure you're far more sensible than I am."

I almost ran back to my bike. My fingers trembled as I unlocked it, then I biked home and stared at our house. Tiny. Red door. A crooked chimney. Next to the weir. It floods every year and the cellar walls are green with slime.

Was it possible?

I grabbed the garden spade and started to dig. I dug all morning. It was hard, sweaty work. Out came those hollyhocks, one by one. I couldn't stop.

And then my spade hit something hard. I scraped away the soil and stones till I could see it was an old green tin box. The lock was so rusty that it broke open as I touched it.

Inside were coins. Masses of gold coins. A fortune. An absolute fortune! I ran my fingers over them. I dabbled my fingers in them.

And under them I found a piece of paper so thick that it was more like heavy old parchment. It was a list of all the coins in the tin box, along with a note that said:

"*This box, and everything inside it, belongs to me.*"

At the bottom was an old, looping signature. *Albert Harper Warren.*

My great-grandfather. The man I was named after, the man who left the house to me and my mum.

I haven't heard his whispering voice again.

Why should I? There's no need. I've found my great-grandfather's fortune.

"Weird," I said. "Really, really weird!"

Laila grinned. "So there you are, Tom!
You *can* get messages from dreams. Messages
that turn out to be true. And I might get the
letter with the good news I dreamed about."

"You might," I said. "And you might have
another dream tonight about a letter with bad
news. That won't be so cheery."

"No," Asim warned her. "You'll feel like
that boy who moved into Number 17 and
found—"

"Stop!" Laila told her brother. "Don't even talk about that horrible story!"

"What horrible story?" I asked.

So Laila put her fingers in her ears, and Asim told me what happened.

Tale 2

The Strange Tale of Number 17

Asim smiled as Laila tugged her hood up over her head and stuck her fingers in her ears. She didn't want to hear the weird story he was going to tell.

But I did, so he turned to me. "You know how creepy Number 17 was," he said. "There was something so weird about the house that no one could stay there. A family would move in on Monday morning. By Friday night they would have left again."

I nodded. I did remember that. They all had different reasons.

Some said, "The house kept turning icy cold."

Some said, "One of the rooms would fill with the most terrible smell."

One parent said, "The children had such bad dreams that they wouldn't go to bed."

Another said, "We heard strange scrabbling noises under the floor."

So now Asim told me the rest of the story ...

*

Nobody wanted to live there. The rent dropped lower and lower, until the house was really cheap. One or two people who had no children moved in. The first gave up on his first day. "I was all right," he said, "but Rusty here wouldn't put a paw inside the place. The hair on his neck stood on end and he just backed away and growled and growled. I tried to drag him in, but he pulled back so hard his head slipped out of his collar. So I gave up. I had moved out even before I moved in!"

A few weeks later, a woman rented the house. On her first morning, she washed the windows and hung new curtains. She even put flower pots outside. She chatted to the people in the house next door.

"This place is perfect for me," she told them. "Perfect! It's so cheap to rent. It's close to my work. I'm going to paint the front door a bright, fresh colour. Yellow, maybe. Or blue. I'm going to settle in and be so happy here."

The next day, she moved out.

The man at Number 19 saw her boxes on the pavement. "What's up?" he said. "You were so keen to stay!"

The woman shuddered. "That was before last night."

He asked, "What happened last night?"

"What *didn't* happen? I went to bed and almost at once the room was icy cold – so cold my breath came out as cloud. I could smell something rotten and heard strange noises from downstairs, as if someone were scrabbling over stones."

She gave herself a little shake. "This house is haunted," she said. "Haunted and unhappy! No one could live here. No one."

And no one did. Nobody even tried until one day a mother and her son stood in front of the house and stared and stared.

The boy's mother asked the man next door, "Why is it empty? The rent's so cheap. It looks like a nice sort of house."

The man next door made up his mind to warn the family. "Number 17 is empty because it's haunted. No one can live there.

Everyone moves in and, hours or days later, they move out again. They just can't stand it."

The boy laughed. "That is so stupid!" he said. "No one believes in ghosts any more. This is the twenty-first century! We have computers and smart phones. Ghosts belong to the past!"

"Cody is right," his mother said. "There are no such things as ghosts! I think we'll rent the house and move in."

"Good luck, then," said the man next door.

Three days later, the family arrived at the house in a car full of boxes. The man from Number 19 watched them unload the boxes on the pavement and unlock the front door to Number 17. Then the man and his wife got back in the car and drove off.

"Mum and Dad have more to pack," the boy said. "They dropped me here to set up my computer stuff."

He picked up the first box. "I'm a computer whizz," he explained. "My name is Cody. My friends call me Computer Cody because I fix all their laptops and smart phones. I can sort almost any computer problem. So if you have any trouble, come round to Number 17."

Computer Cody carried all his boxes into the house and shut the door behind him. He unpacked his large flat screen and sets of speakers. He rooted in other boxes for odd plugs and wires, and fitted them together. In the last box, he found an electric kettle, a tin of hot chocolate, a packet of biscuits and his big red mug, all wrapped in newspaper.

Cody grinned. "A little surprise to keep me going!" he said. "Good old Mum and Dad!"

He settled down to get sorted.

First he set up his computer. He added his speakers and router and went to his email. The first to come up was from a friend from school, but it was hard to read. The letters seemed to shiver on the screen.

"Maybe a loose connection," Cody muttered. He got down on his knees to make sure all his plugs were firmly in their sockets. He checked the switches and wires. He even folded a piece of paper into four and slid it under the desk leg to stop any rocking.

The letters on the screen still looked so pale and shivery.

"That's not the best this screen can do," Cody said firmly. He remembered the photos he'd seen of 17 Weir Street when his family were making up their minds to rent it. They had been clear as fresh paint.

"I'll find those photos again," he told himself. "I can remember how they looked. So that will be a good test of whether my system is working."

He cleared the screen and typed in *17 Weir Street.*

Up came a photo of the house. But it looked different. More grey. Much more blurred. Almost fuzzy. It didn't look like the sort of photo that would be on a website of homes to rent. It looked more like something he'd see in his great-grandma's photo album.

Cody leaned forward. How strange! It hardly looked like the same house. Even the windows looked different. The windows behind him in the room where he was now were not at all like those on the screen. Those were the old sort you had to slide up. He swung round on his chair to check. Yes. He was right. The windows behind him were the new kind that opened outwards.

Then Cody spotted something else. The house on the screen had smoke drifting from a chimney. Cody looked round. There was no fireplace.

Perhaps that was in another room. Puzzled, Cody slid off his chair and went all round the house.

There was no fireplace in any room, upstairs or down.

Strange ...

Cody went back to peer at the photo on his screen. This time, he saw yet another thing that was different. Down at street level the photo showed a small window with bars across it.

Had the house once had a cellar? Or one of those old coal holes?

Cody went to the front door and stepped out. He walked across the street and turned back to look at Number 17.

No cellar. No coal hole. Not even that tiny window. And yet it must have been there once because Cody could see an ugly little patch of brick where someone had filled it in.

"And done a rubbish job," Cody said to himself. "As if they bricked it up in a big hurry."

Cody went back to his computer and looked again. There was no way this was the photo he had seen before! The one on the website had been far more recent, and there'd been no tiny window at the level of the street.

"This is so *weird*," said Cody.

He pressed *Refresh*.

Up came the same old photo. But this time, up against the bars of the tiny window was a pale oval smudge.

Was it a *face*? A child's face?

Cody stared at the photo. That face hadn't been there before! Was it a problem with the computer? Or was it him? Was he doing stupid things?

He typed *17 Weir Street* again.

Up flashed the image of a child. Cody could see more this time, as if the computer had zoomed in. The child was so small – no more than five or six years old. He wore a torn old nightgown and had the saddest face. Cody felt as if the little boy was staring into his eyes.

"Creepy!" Cody muttered. This time he closed the screen page carefully. As soon as the image was gone, he typed the words for the third time – *17 Weir Street*.

Up came the child. Now he looked even sadder and thinner. The nightgown was dirty – almost black – and he was holding out a hand, as if to beg for help.

A chill ran down Cody's skin. He stared round the room, but everything looked so *normal*. A chair. A desk. His boxes of computer stuff. A normal room for a normal boy.

"Stop it!" he told himself. "You're just imagining things because of what that man next door said. Look at something else!"

He went back to the email from his friend. The letters still looked pale and shivery, but he could read them. *Did the move go OK?*

Move went fine, Cody wrote back. *Free now. Want to meet up?*

He looked up. On the screen the spell check had taken over. It had underlined the word *free* and suggested **Trapped** instead.

Trapped?

'Odd ...' Cody thought. He deleted the suggestion and typed to his friend:

I'm hungry.

Up came the spell check again. This time it had underlined the word *hungry* and suggested **Starving**.

Cody ignored the spell check. He typed:

We could eat pizza.

This time, the spell check underlined *pizza* and suggested **Coal**.

Coal?

Trapped? Starving? Coal?

Cody stared around the room. "Think!" he said softly. "Think!"

But there was only one thing to think. A haunted house. A cellar with a window that someone had bricked up. A trapped child so hungry that he'd eaten coal.

Cody pushed back his chair and went to find the page of newspaper his mum and dad had used to wrap his snack and mug. He laid it flat. *The Milford Gazette*. To have a name like that, the paper must have been around for years and years.

But even local newspapers had all their old copies online now.

Cody found the *Milford Gazette* website on his computer. He keyed in *17 Weir Street* and pressed *Search*.

Up came the story, dated 2 June 1902.

SEARCH GOES ON FOR MISSING CHILD

Family, police and neighbours kept up their search for little Peter Lane, aged 4. Peter went missing from his home at 17 Weir Street

two weeks ago today. His father, Walter Lane, wept as he told *The Milford Gazette*, "Our little Peter has been deaf and dumb from birth. He can't call for help or hear when people call. Everyone has helped to look for him. We've searched all over. But now we have to face the fact that something terrible must have happened after he vanished from the house. Perhaps he went too near the weir and—

Cody stopped reading.

As soon as he stopped trembling, he picked up his phone.

His mum answered almost at once. "Cody? We're on our way. Are you all right?"

"Mum," Cody said. His voice shook. "Mum, we have to phone the police."

*

A few weeks later, there was a funeral. It was simple and quick. After it, Cody and his parents walked back to the car park with the police officer who had come round to the house after they made the phone call. She'd listened to the story. Together, she and Cody's father had lifted a corner of the carpet in one room after another until they found the trap door.

It was nailed shut.

Together, the police officer and Cody's father had forced it open. They went down the cellar steps and slid back the bolt on a big heavy door.

Behind it, in the cold and dark, they found what they expected.

The body of a child.

Now, on the way back from the funeral, Cody said, "What do you think really

happened? Was it an accident? Or something more sinister?"

The police officer shook her head. "We'll never know," she said. "That poor child was deaf and dumb. And only four. Even if he stood on the pile of coal, he probably couldn't reach up high enough to bang on the floor above." She gave a little shiver. "Imagine! Months pass with no word. Then one day it's cold enough for a fire. The father lifts the trap door. He goes down the cellar steps and unbolts the door." The police officer shivered. "If I'd seen what he saw ..."

"Yes," Cody said. "If you'd seen what he saw ...?"

"I might not have been able to face the world," the police officer admitted. "Or face the truth. I might have rushed back up the steps and lied to my family. I might have said, 'I'm sick of coal fires! Dirty, messy things!

Let's buy a paraffin heater! Today! Before winter sets in!'"

The police officer bit her lip. "I can see why I might have nailed down the trap door so no one would ever see what I had seen. I might have taken out the fireplace. Anything that might remind me. Even bricked up that tiny window so people would forget there had ever been a coal cellar there."

She shrugged. "There is one good thing," she went on. "Now it's all over, you'll be able to stay."

"Oh no, we won't," said Cody's father. "We're moving out on Friday. It's all organised."

The police officer was surprised. "But that child's had a proper funeral now," she said. "He'll be at peace. The house won't be haunted any more."

"Not for the next people, maybe," Cody's mother said.

And Cody agreed. "No. They won't spend their whole lives asking themselves exactly what happened all those long years ago." He sighed. "But 17 Weir Street will always be haunted for me."

I waved my hands in front of Laila's face. She pulled her fingers out of her ears and pushed back her hood.

I told her, "It's safe to listen now. Asim has finished. But I can see why you didn't want to hear that story a second time!"

Laila said, "I know the house isn't haunted any more. The family in there are happy and never say a word about anything creepy. But I still can't walk past without a shiver."

We all stared up the street. "It looks like such a *normal* house," Asim said. "You don't expect the ghost of a little boy to haunt a house like that."

"Yes, it looks almost a *boring* house," agreed Laila.

Asim went on, "You expect a ghost to live in a house more like those at the top of our street. Like that grand old tumble-down house with the big garden that's hidden behind those high walls. You know – the one where those three children come to stay in the holidays."

"I went to play with them one day," I said. "Ages ago. And maybe that house is haunted too, because I remember they told me a very strange story."

"Go on, Tom," said Laila. "Tell us."

So I told them the third and last story.

Tale 3

The Boy in the Greenhouse

The children at that big house told me they loved to pretend that their granny's home was haunted. And it was the perfect house for that. The curtains were so old and thick that every room was gloomy. The back stairs were dark and crooked. Doors creaked when you opened or closed them, and every corner of every room seemed to have its own spider web.

Their granny would say, "There's nothing wrong with this house. It's just old and drab and tired – the way I'll be one day!"

But Rosa, Ruben and Silvia wanted to pretend that it was horribly haunted. They'd beg to leave the table at the end of meals.

They'd hurry out of the wide doors onto the lawn. They'd pick their way along the path under the arches of roses. "Ouch! Mind that bit! So many thorns!" Behind a line of high, dark bushes was an old stable block. The horses were long gone, but as the children came closer, black ravens would fly up in circles round their heads.

Rosa would shiver. "Ravens!"

"The most creepy bird of all," Ruben agreed.

Behind the stables there was a high wall, and set in that was an old wooden door that hung off its hinges.

One by one the children would squeeze through the gap into the old kitchen garden where fruit and vegetables and herbs used to grow in neat little plots. Now it was a sea of tangles.

At the far end was a greenhouse. Most of the glass had fallen out years ago. The empty metal frames that were left were red with rust. Inside, most of the wooden ledges on which so many heavy plant pots used to stand were weak and rotten.

No one grew anything in there any more, but it still smelled of greenhouse – rich and earthy and damp.

The children tried to give each other the shivers.

"Someone has been in here since yesterday," Ruben would whisper to his sisters. "I'm sure that plant pot wasn't there before."

Rosa would spin round. "Did you see that? A shadow flitted past the door!"

Silvia would cup a hand to her ear. "I'm sure I can hear someone weeping."

It was a game they played for hours. Their granny would call them in for supper, then send them up to wash, and clean their teeth, and get into their beds. But still they didn't stop the game. The three of them would kneel in a line along the bench below a window sill upstairs and stare out into the dark.

"Look! A strange green light in the stable block!"

"Something in white just floated across the corner of the lawn!"

"Someone is wailing as if their heart would break."

Granny would call up, "Go to bed! All of you! Now!"

And in the end they did. But it was only so that they could get up even earlier in the morning. The three of them would creep out of the house before their granny was awake to see the lines of footprints they had left across the lawn in the dew.

Playing the game again, day after day.

On the very last morning of the holiday, the children slipped out of the house before breakfast as usual. But as they came closer to the greenhouse, they saw a boy sitting on an old seed box. His back was turned, but they could see he was about the same age as Ruben. He wore grey shorts and a grey jumper that made him look as if he was in his school uniform.

But this was the middle of the summer holidays.

The children knew that their granny was friendly with many of the families who lived nearby. Perhaps, thought Ruben, she knew this boy, and had invited him to come and play in her enormous garden any time he wanted.

It would, Ruben thought, be good to have another boy to join their game.

Ruben walked closer. Even before he said "Hello", the boy had turned to face them. Across his forehead was a deep red scar that ran up under his fringe.

Ruben tried not to stare. Instead, he said the first thing that came to mind. "Are you waiting for someone?"

The boy smiled. "Not really, no. I was just sitting here, thinking about things."

Silvia was far too young to know which sort of questions it was polite to ask, and which were nosy. "What things?" she demanded.

"Just things," said the boy.

"So what's your name?"

The boy stuck out his hand. "Rupert."

"*Rupert?*" repeated Silvia. She sounded as if she'd never heard the name before and wasn't sure she'd got it right.

"Yes, Rupert," the boy said. As if he guessed that Silvia hadn't yet learned how to shake hands, he let his arm drop. "And you are ...?"

"Silvia," said Silvia. "This," she said, pointing, "is my sister Rosa. And this is my brother Ruben."

"We play round here a lot," said Ruben, "but we've never seen you before."

Rupert just shrugged. Rosa was about to ask him where he came from when Silvia broke in. "Yes, we play here a lot because it's so *creepy*. The stable is full of broken things that nobody has wanted for years and years. And down here in the old greenhouse, creepers hang over everything and there are shadows in every corner. The glass panes rattle, the doors creak in the wind, and ravens sit and watch us. It is the perfect place for ghosts."

Rupert gave Silvia a smile. "You know that there are no such things as ghosts."

"But we *pretend*," said Silvia. "Sometimes we do that all day long. We pretend that we've seen ladies in long white dresses flit along the hall or round corners. We pretend we can hear the wails and moans of dead children. We pretend that the ghosts have been in here while we've been out, and moved some things around and broken others."

The boy called Rupert looked puzzled. "But, Silvia, I just told you. There are no such things as ghosts."

Rosa frowned. What was this strange boy's problem? Silvia had *said* that it was only a game.

Now Silvia looked puzzled too. Hadn't he understood? "It's only make-believe," she explained again kindly. "We make it all up as we go along."

Rosa backed her sister up. "Yes. Silvia loves the game, and so we play it with her."

Silvia was upset. She said to her brother and sister, "Both of you like to play it too!"

Rosa looked at Ruben, who stared at his feet. They didn't want to tell a boy the same age as them that they enjoyed a silly game that made them shiver. But it was true. And these were the very last hours that they could spend in Granny's garden before they had to go home.

Why waste a whole day just because of a boy who couldn't tell the difference between real and pretend?

"Come on," Rosa said to Rupert. "Try it! Join in and see."

"All right," said Rupert. "How do we start?"

So Rosa and Ruben tried to explain the game. But it was hopeless. Hopeless! It was as if Rupert had never heard of pretending. He kept saying things like, "But if you don't really hear someone crying, why would you say you did?" And, "But if you don't really see a strange shadow flit across the lawn, why point and call to the others?"

In the end, Rosa and Ruben gave up. "Let's just get on and play," Rosa said. "You'll pick it up."

Ruben squeezed back through the gap by the old door in the wall. The others followed. He stood in the shadow of the yew tree and pointed across the lawn. "You see the statue of the mermaid?"

Silvia pointed. "The one beside the little goldfish pond?"

"Yes," Ruben said. "Well, I was staring at her yesterday, and suddenly she moved her tail. Only a tiny bit. But she really did move it!"

Silvia and Rosa were into the game at once. They stared at the statue for a few seconds, then Silvia said, "Yes! Look! The mermaid rolled her tail. Not much. But I still saw it."

Rosa pointed, "Look! She's moving it again!"

Rupert stared at the statue. Then he turned back to say, "But that's impossible! That statue is made of stone. No bits of it can move."

"Remember," Silvia told him, "we are *pretending*."

They went to a different part of the garden and tried again. The four of them lay under the bushes to watch the mossy path that ran around the house.

"What are we waiting for?" asked Rupert.

"Not what," whispered Silvia. "*Who?*" She turned back to stare at the path, then flung out her arm. "See? See that pale lady coming down the path? Her feet aren't touching the ground. She's floating in the air. She's *floating*."

"But who can she be?" Rosa whispered.

"Oh, some unhappy ghost," Ruben answered. "I expect she's floating down the very same path she took on the last walk of her sad life."

"Nonsense!" said Rupert. He didn't whisper like the others. He spoke quite loudly. "This is nonsense! I told you. There are no such things as ghosts."

Ruben had had enough. He got to his feet. "Come on, Rosa," he said. "Come along, Silvia. We have to go back to the house now." He turned to Rupert. "It was fun to meet you. But now we need to get back to our granny. She will be waiting for us."

Rosa knew why he was saying what he did. But Silvia didn't.

"*Why* are we going back so soon?" she wailed. "We normally stay out in the garden much longer. What's different about today?"

Ruben waited till all three of them were in the house before he said, "I'll tell you what's different, Silvia. That *Rupert* is different. And he was spoiling the game."

"Totally spoiling it!" Rosa agreed. "He hasn't any idea how to pretend. It was a complete waste of time trying to explain. I hope he soon pushes off home."

The children went upstairs to peer out of one of the windows. There was no sign of Rupert in the garden.

"We'll wait another half an hour," Rosa suggested. "Just in case. And then we can go out and play the game again."

On their way back down the stairs, they met their granny in the hall. She was carrying an old hat box with faded stripes. As soon as she saw them, she put the box down and looked at her watch. "Well, this is a surprise! The three of you are normally still outside at this time."

"We will be again soon," said Rosa. She didn't want to tell her granny that they were hiding from the strange new boy. After all, their granny must have invited him into the garden to play. Instead, she asked, "What are you doing, Granny?   What's in the box?"

"Photos," said Granny.

Silvia said, "Are they photos of people we know?"

Granny smiled down at her. "Yes, Silvia. Some of them will be people you know. It's a box of old family photos."

"So can we see?" begged Silvia.

"Why not?" said Granny.

She took the box into the dining room and tipped the photos out on the table. They slid over the polished wood. The children picked them up, one by one, to look at them.

"Who's this?" asked Rosa. She pointed to a young woman in bright yellow trousers who sat, smiling, on a swing.

"That's me," said Granny.

Rosa was astonished. *"You?"*

Granny said, "Everyone was young once, Rosa! Even me."

Ruben picked up another of the photos. It was a tall, thin man in smart army uniform. "And who is this?"

"That's your great-grandfather," said Granny. "That photo was taken on the day he went to join his regiment."

"To go to war?" asked Rosa.

"Yes," Granny said. "To go to war."

"Did he come back safely?" asked Silvia.

"Yes," Granny said. "He was lucky." She sighed. "And that was such a good thing because, while he was away at war, his younger brother died."

Silvia was horrified. "Died? How?"

"It was an accident," Granny said sadly. "The poor lad was only ten when his horse threw him down by the old stables. He hit his head on a stone. There was a gash from here to here."

She drew a line with her finger across her forehead, right up into her hair. "And after that," she said, "he seemed fine for a day or two. The wound was healing. But he was not himself at all. His mother kept saying, 'There's something wrong with him. He isn't right!' And then, a few days later, a fever took him and he died."

The children were silent. Only ten years old? Almost their own age.

Granny said, "It was a terrible business. Everyone said he was a lovely young lad before the accident. Wait! I can show you."

She picked up photos till she found the one she wanted. She slid it over the table so all three children could see it. A boy in grey shorts and a grey jumper waved cheerily at the camera.

Silvia stared. "Rupert!"

"Yes, Rupert!" Rosa echoed.

Now it was Granny's turn to be astonished. "How do you know his name?"

Ruben said quietly, "We met him. Only this morning. He was in the garden until we came inside."

"In the garden?" Granny looked so confused. "But that's impossible!"

"He was there," said Silvia. "We let him play with us, but he was no good at pretending. He just kept saying there were

no such things as ghosts. 'Nonsense!' he kept
on telling us. 'That's just nonsense!'"

They all fell quiet. Then Granny shivered. She reached across to gather up the photos and drop them back in the box.

"I think that I shall sort them out another day," she told the children. Her voice was shaky. "Right now, let's have our breakfast."

"Please," Silvia said. "Yes, please. Something that's plain and real and not at all creepy. Our breakfast."

"Then we must go upstairs and pack our stuff," said Rosa.

"Yes," Ruben said. He tried to hide his great relief. "Because this is our last day. Soon we'll be going home."

"Well, Tom," Laila said firmly, "that was the spookiest story of all."

"*All* the stories were spooky," said Asim. "Three different sorts of spooky."

I nodded. Asim and Laila were right. The stories were three different sorts of spooky. But all of them were about houses along our road.

No wonder we call it Weird Street.

I think we always will.

Our books are tested
for children and young people by
children and young people.

Thanks to everyone who consulted on
a manuscript for their time and effort in
helping us to make our books better
for our readers.